7

Grimm's
Fairy Tales

For Uncle Max
S.P.

For Olivia
C.J.

ORCHARD BOOKS
338 Euston Road, London NW1 3BH
Orchard Books Australia
Level 17/207 Kent Street, Sydney, NSW 2000

This text was first published in the form of a gift collection called
The Sleeping Princess by Orchard Books in 2002

This edition first published in hardback in 2012
First paperback publication in 2013

ISBN 978 1 40830 837 0 (hardback)
ISBN 978 1 40830 838 7 (paperback)

Text © Saviour Pirotta 2002
Illustrations © Cecilia Johansson 2012

The rights of Saviour Pirotta to be identified as the author and
Cecilia Johansson to be identified as the illustrator of this work
have been asserted by them in accordance
with the Copyright, Designs and Patents Act, 1988.

A CIP catalogue record for this book is available
from the British Library.

1 3 5 7 9 10 8 6 4 2 (hardback)
1 3 5 7 9 10 8 6 4 2 (paperback)

Printed in China

Orchard Books is a division of Hachette Children's Books,
an Hachette UK company.
www.hachette.co.uk

Grimm's Fairy Tales

Little Mouse and Lazy Cat

Written by Saviour Pirotta

Illustrated by Cecilia Johansson

ORCHARD

Once there was a naughty old cat who made friends with a mouse. The two of them decided to set up house together.

"The first thing we must do," said the cat, "is to save some food for the winter. That way we won't starve when it starts to snow and there are no scraps to be found on the street."

The mouse agreed, so the two of them counted all their money and bought a very large pot of fat.

"Where shall we hide it?" asked the mouse.

"Let's bury it in the church," replied the cat.
"No one ever dares steal anything from there."

So the cat and the mouse buried the precious pot of fat under the altar in the church.

Then the mouse set about making their new home all spick-and-span.

The cat didn't do any work at all. She just lazed about in the sun, her mouth watering at the thought of the delicious pot of fat under the altar.

So she said to the mouse, "Would you mind looking after the house by yourself tomorrow? I've just heard from my cousin who's had a new kitten."

The cat continued, "She's asked me to be godmother at the christening. I couldn't say no – the baby is brown with white spots."

"You should go then," said the mouse.

Early the next morning, the cat went off
to the church. There was no christening,
of course; the cat had lied. When no one
was looking, she crept behind the altar
and dug up the pot of fat.

Greedily, she stuck in her paw and licked the fat off her fur. *Mmmm . . .* it was delicious.

The cat ate more and more until she had creamed off the top.

Then she put the pot back under the altar . . .

. . . and went to visit her friends. She didn't
return home until very late.

"What did they call the kitten at the
christening?" asked the mouse.

"Top-Off," said the cat, her mind still on the pot of fat.

"What a strange name," said the mouse.

"Yes, indeed," said the cat, and got into bed.

Barely a week had passed before the cat
started longing for more of the fat.

Once again, the cat said to the mouse, "You won't believe this, but my other sister has had a new kitten too. She's asked me to be the godmother. The new kitten is so pretty with a white ring around her neck. I just couldn't say no."

The mouse agreed to look after the house
while the cat was gone. The next day the cat
crept off to the church a second time.

There she dug up the pot and, before she could stop herself, gobbled up half the fat. *Mmmm* . . . it was delicious!

When the cat could eat no more, she buried the half-empty pot and set off to see her friends. She waited until the moon had risen in the sky before she went home.

"And what did they call this one?" asked the mouse.

"Half-Finished," replied the cat.

"Half-Finished?" said the mouse, suspiciously. "I've never heard that name before. I'll bet my tail there's no saint in heaven with that name."

A few days passed and the cat could hardly sleep for thinking about the pot.

At last she said to the mouse, "It seems that good things come in threes, for yet another of my sisters has given birth to a kitten."

The cat left the house straightaway. "She too has asked me to be godmother. I can't refuse as the little one has black fur and white paws," the cat called to the mouse.

"Top-Off, Half-Finished," mumbled the mouse. "They're such odd names, I don't know what to believe. But off you go, then."

Once more the cat pitter-pattered to the church and dug up the pot.

Before you could say "whiskers", the fat was all gone. Then the cat went to celebrate with her friends. As before, she waited until it was dark and the sky was full of stars before returning home.

"And what have they called this child?"
asked the mouse straightaway.

"All-Gone," said the cat, without stopping
to think.

"That's the strangest name yet!" exclaimed
the mouse. "I'm sure you've made it up,
although I have no idea why."

Time passed and autumn turned into winter. Soon there was no food to be found outside.

The mouse and the cat set off to the church to dig up the pot. It was, of course, empty.

"I see what's been going on!" cried the mouse, shaking with rage. "You've been coming here to eat the fat while you were supposed to be at those christenings. I should have known not to trust a cat! First Top-Off, then Half-Finished and finally—"

"All-Gone!" roared the cat. And she leapt on the poor little mouse and gobbled her up in one go. *Mmmm* . . . she was delicious.

Sometimes life is not fair at all!